THE SKY ABOVE

ESSENTIAL POETS SERIES 310

Canada Council   Conseil des Arts
for the Arts   du Canada

ONTARIO ARTS COUNCIL
CONSEIL DES ARTS DE L'ONTARIO

an Ontario government agency
un organisme du gouvernement de l'Ont

Canada

Guernica Editions Inc. acknowledges the support of the Canada Council
for the Arts and the Ontario Arts Council. The Ontario Arts Council
is an agency of the Government of Ontario.

We acknowledge the financial support of the Government of Canada.

MARTY GERVAIS

THE SKY ABOVE

GUERNICA
EDITIONS

TORONTO – CHICAGO – BUFFALO – LANCASTER (U.K.)

2024

Guernica Founder: Antonio D'Alfonso

Michael Mirolla, general editor
John B. Lee & Bruce Meyer, editors
Cover and interior design: Errol F. Richardson
Cover image: Linda Goodhue

Guernica Editions Inc.
1241 Marble Rock Rd., Gananoque, (ON), Canada K7G 2V4
2250 Military Road, Tonawanda, N.Y. 14150-6000 U.S.A.
www.guernicaeditions.com

Distributors:
University of Toronto Press Distribution (UTP)
5201 Dufferin Street, Toronto (ON), Canada M3H 5T8
Independent Publishers Group (IPG)
814 N Franklin Street, Chicago, IL 60610, U.S.A.

First edition.
Printed in Canada.

Legal Deposit – Third Quarter
Library of Congress Catalogue Card Number: 2024930446
Library and Archives Canada Cataloguing in Publication
Title: The sky above : a selected / Marty Gervais.
Names: Gervais, C. H. (Charles Henry), 1946- author.
Series: Essential poets ; 310.
Description: First edition. | Series statement: Essential poets series ; 310
Identifiers: Canadiana 20240287126 | ISBN 9781771838726 (softcover)
Subjects: LCGFT: Poetry.
Classification: LCC PS8563.E7 S59 2024 | DDC C811/.54—dc23

This book is for Donna

Contents

Foreword

The role of the poet is to express the humanity of the people, places, and experiences he loves. Samuel Johnson said that a poet must be a keen observer of everything in his world, a statement reminiscent of the New York Yankee's catcher Yogi Berra: "You can observe a lot by watching." It is not hard to imagine the poet behind the poems in this volume as someone who enters the world with a journalist's notepad in his hand, someone constantly hungry, not for a sensational story, but for a human one.

My pleasure in this book, aside from the delight I find in the craft of Marty Gervais's work, is the profound engagement that springs from them. Gervais takes us to moments in his life as he saw them and sees them. I have had the pleasure of knowing Gervais for five decades. He discovered me when I was a young, unpublished poet and brought me into print. Each time we meet, I marvel at his range of experience, his natural ability not only to tell a story but to spot the value and joy of being alive in the moments Gervais shares.

The poems in this volume are Gervais's best work as selected by our mutual friend and poet, John B. Lee. I wanted to honour the poems by allowing each one to speak for itself. I wanted the craft and delicacy Gervais expresses to shine through. No other arrangement would do them the justice they deserve. This book is meant to be read as a portal into a beautiful, thoughtful, and loving mind as Gervais takes us on a journey through the world he loves. As the Medieval mystic, Richard Rolle, noted, "People become like what they love." This is a book of love letters Gervais has written to the world and I know you will love them as much as I do.

Bruce Meyer

Bringing the Place to Life: A Preface

Marty Gervais is a poet who believes in the power of story, and as storyteller he confirms his faith in poetry in every line. It should come as no surprise to anyone who reads his work that he has spent most of his working life as an award-winning journalist. He is also a first-rate photographer, a consummate editor, a formidable literary publisher, and a champion of fellow authors throughout Canada. He's a chronicler of the many lives he's touched. He weaves in and out of the landscape where he lives like the dapple of light and shade in the chiaroscuro of an artist's pen, like the sunlight and cloud-shadow in the gentle caress of watercolour that barely blushes the page in natural perfection. In a poem that comes early in this wonderful book he writes of his aspiration as "a way of making sense, a finding of purpose, or maybe it's a search for something undefinable, inaccessible" (lines from his poem "Geography of Every Day").

His commitment to poetry began one day in his youth when a teacher first introduced him to the sonnets of Shakespeare. His imagination came alive. And what a blessing that event. It would not be an exaggeration to claim that Gervais is one of the premier poets of his generation. We who live in Souwesto are grateful for the presence of a chronicler of our place and time. Like Falkner's Mississippi, Laurence's prairie home, we have a poet who cherishes and reifies this landscape, this region, our home.

John B. Lee, Poet Laureate of the City of Brantford,
Norfolk County

In three words I can sum up everything I've learned about life:
it goes on ...
—Robert Frost

There's nothing more extraordinary than reality ...
—Mary Ellen Mark

... Look at that face, look at the gesture that someone makes,
look at the way the light rolls across the land ...
the pleasure of seeing ...
—Joel Meyerowitz

Geography of Every Day

I wake in the morning, pretending
this is all new, that I have landed
in a foreign country and the only things
familiar are my watch and hearing aids
nearby on a table, a novel, a set of keys
wallet and two fountain pens

but this is home, and the dream
I have tumbled out of is a way
of making sense or finding purpose
or maybe it's a search for something
undefinable, inaccessible

Yet I am home, and around me
is the geography of every day
a sweater slung over the foot board
of the double bed my wife bought
when she was in high school

a dresser across the room cluttered
with things never put away

the blinds in the two windows
pulled down but leaking streams
of June's exquisite daylight

I am home — this is only me

Hands

The first
— those that snatched me
from my mother and lifted me
into the light to my father
in a cold corridor
at Metropolitan Hospital

From that point on,
my life was one of
adult hands — a school nun
gripping my wrist
as she wielded a leather strap

doctors tilting my chin, palms
flat against my forehead
to find a fever

a priest's rough hands offering
to place the eucharist upon
my gaping tongue

teachers sliding my fingers
off a page to check the scratchings
of additions and subtractions

many years later my dear mother
just before she died
gently cupping my hands
like two tiny doves

and promising she
would bake me a pie

The Magic Wand

for Lucien

The wizard is poised in the room
like a Halloween witch
with that wide-brimmed peaked hat
prattling on like a philosopher
inviting us to feel that invisible ball of energy
vibrating between our outstretched hands

She's here for the launch of the new Harry Potter book
but my five-year-old grandson is lost
in the magic wand she has placed in his hands
as she speaks about drawing protectives circles
casting spells, warding off dark forces
even banishing bunions

My grandson marvels at this instrument
whispering feverishly "Abracadabra … abracadabra …"
— no longer hearing this wizard
who has fashioned this shaman's wand
from an aging oak tree

Instead, he's channeling his own energy into the room
but it isn't working, nothing is flying about
no sudden gusts of wind, nor pantry doors
slamming shut, nor teacups rattling in mid air
and nothing bigger than he might imagine:

still poverty, still a need for world peace
still violence and pestilence and polluted lakes

My grandson is poised and ready
and frantically waves the wand about him
like a symphonic conductor gone mad

yet nothing changes — it won't even silence
this nattering witch from telling us
about Greco Roman wands
or ceremonial fire wands and lotus wands
or those used by the freemasons in
all their ritualistic nonsense

then suddenly in a dramatic abracadabra ending
my grandson shatters the spell:
"Hey, lady, how does this thing work?"

Under the Weight of Heaven

For Brother Paul Quenon at the Abbey of Gethsemani

You sleep in the tool shed
by the road under the stars
at the back of the monastery
and tell me about the lovers
— the farm boys
with their sweethearts
who steal into the night
when all are asleep here
and park their cars
in the holy stillness
and after a while
quietly drive back out
to the highway
You hear their cars
mounting the hill beyond
and hear them disappear into
the splendid darkness
You sleep in the tool shed
by the road under the stars
and awake suddenly to
an unfamiliar sound
and look up and see
the enormous shape
of a horse like a mountain
emerging from the mist
in the early morning
but only a horse
a mare that has strayed from
a nearby farm

It lolls about
under the swaying weight
of the heavens
You sleep in the tool shed
by the road
under the stars
and wake to the morning
with the bells beckoning you
to vigils — then you see
this work horse lying
in the dark meadow
and nod to her as you would
a friend, and say Good morning
then make your way to chapel

You sleep in the tool shed
under the stars
where the world
comes to you
— silent guests who steal away
your sleep, who leave you
wondering, who leave you
undisturbed, alone

You sleep in the tool shed
under the weight of Heaven ...

Breathing Sweet Hope

I sit in my car
by the side of the road
watch the combine
shave this field of winter wheat
golden and flat under a dreamy
dark summer sky
I am going to make some changes
That farmer will be my grandfather
He will float over
this landscape — straw hat
coveralls, pipe clenched
in his teeth
I will have him wave to me
from where I sit at the road's edge
I will shift the barns
and chicken coop and outhouse
closer to the house
haul out the wagons
and have my grandfather lead
the work horses into the farm yard
I will put back the oak trees
cut down years ago
in that empty pasture
where we picnicked after church
I will be six again
lumber in a summer storm
and hurry my grandmother
across the yard to shut
the enormous barn doors
against wind and rain

I will put laughter
back into her mouth
as she scoops up my limp body
that has collapsed abruptly
because the sky has erupted
into sudden thunder
I will paint reflections
in her glasses that show
wind swept trees
and spooked barn owls
as we race back to the house
I will exchange the words
in my grandfather's frown
as he stands by the back steps
to tell my mother
who has driven an hour
in the still-dark morning
to hear him say
"Ta mere est morte."
Instead, my grandmother
will be in the kitchen
loading the wood stove
and turning to my mother
and holding her for that instant
I will stop time
— here and now — to move
all these pieces into place
the perfect farm life
in this imagined game
I will open the eyes of those I love
and breathe sweet hope
into their limbs and words
I will let prayers
finally have their day

Mother

I see that girl born
in the back bedroom of that farm
that sits tall on a landscape
that gives itself to rain and sun

I hear her tiny voice
bearing itself clean like an echo
in the upstairs corridors
her mother holding her close

daytime breaking over wheat fields
and furrowed and flat terrain, and I hear
her father's steps on the wooden stairs
as he moves to greet his baby daughter

You would be 100 today
if you had not died at the hospital
on the 5th floor where
the morning sun poured in

I raced up the stairs
and along the corridor to your room

your mouth gaping open
as if to swallow the ceiling above
spectacles on the night table
glimmering in mute sunlight

I was too late to say goodbye

Today I say hello, your birthday
You would be 100

MARTY GERVAIS

When the Light Gets Warm

When the light gets warm
the world curves
around the Stoney Point farmhouse
where childhood races in sunlight
disappearing into shadows

I am a boy hiding
on my brothers in the henhouse
peering through chicken wire
to the yard with
its shiny bright blue Buick
I see them running
trying to find me
I am giggling
and the birds
cautiously step away
like 11-year-old girls
walking in an older sister's
high heels

When the light gets warm
I am a boy squatting
in the henhouse
watching the day wind
down, seeing my family
search behind
farm sheds, silos
and along fence rows
I see my mother pushing
back a lock of hair

26

one hand on her hip
in worry, my father
pacing beside the car
and lighting up a cigarette
my grandmother coming
from the house, the screen door
slapping behind her
wanting the last word

When the light gets warm
they have given up
and no longer call out
and my father slips into the Buick
slams the door and
my brothers pile in one by one
so does my mother
who glances back
one last time
I feel so alone as
I sit in the henhouse
and wonder at my hands
cupping a heart full of melancholy
knowing summer is
turning to twilight

When the light gets warm
I suddenly burst
from the henhouse
my six-year-old legs
sprinting to the Buick
that is now moving
in a cloud of road dust
and I can smell

the fields of wheat
and hear my tiny voice
rising all the way up
from my beating heart
in my chest
then see a back door
opening and a brother's hand
reaching out …

Shooting Dogs

I never could shoot the coyotes
though I joined my neighbours
who tracked and hunted them down
through wind-swept winter fields of Essex County
I rode with those farmers in the cabs of
bumpy smoky pickups, windows wide open
rifles tucked beside, the trucks racing
along concession roads as we drove
herding those coyotes across stubbled fields

I watched these hunters pile out
of their trucks to file alongside the road
lined up like soldiers — cold rifles
trained on the coyotes, and one by one
these doomed creatures rushed into
their gun-sights, tumbling and squealing

but one coyote sped between the lineup
raced past the trucks into the open flats and beyond
as the farmers followed, each raising his rifle
but the wind was strong and they let that brush wolf go —
and I watched it disappear into
the far off snowy field's horizon running
for all its life, never once looking back

When I turned around, I saw the men
lighting up cigars, rifles balanced on forearms
celebrating their victory before moving
into the late windy afternoon to collect the kill
and toss each carcass into the bed of their pickups

Later I stopped by a neighbour's barn
surprised to see these stiff-bodied coyotes
dangling from hooks
and photographed them for the paper
and heard startling tales of how these animals
raided chicken coops, dragged off family pets
you name the harm they'd done ...

and I snapped a dozen pictures, moving in and out
and around and through the cold barn, half listening
to the chatter among the men drinking beer
and thought *I'm really no better than them*
— *I'm shooting coyotes too*

Finally I left, just as daylight faded
and hopped into my car, felt it shudder, then start
and headed home to a spit-gray cold January sky
daydreaming and feeling low, and was maybe
a half mile from my place, and started fiddling
with the radio to tune in the news
when out of the corner of my eye
there was a coyote crouching
at the edge of the ditch

I stopped, lowered my window
— the lone coyote didn't budge — I studied
his narrow, elongated snout, lean body
bushy tail, thick fur, and his yellow eyes
— I dared not take his picture

Letters Home From a Mountie Recruit

for my brother Ted

I can't forget your letters home
postmarked *Regina, Sask*
neatly folded, handwritten, stuffed
into fat envelopes and arriving
at the post office at the end of summer 1961
and our mother seated at the kitchen table
the back door open to morning sunlight
and hearing your voice in hers
as she read about
those first days in training —

new recruits jarred from a dead asleep
by a drill sergeant on a cold and windy day
to run at dawn under a canopy of storm clouds —
the vast open landscape like an empty
tabletop stretched out before you
and making you believe maybe
the world was flat after all

and the day after you arrived
I imagine you sat on the edge
of your bunk bed and hurried to pull on
a pair of stiff riding boots
before filing out to the stables
and my mind slipped easily
into that instant trying to relive it

the moment, too, when first you saw
those towering black thoroughbreds
1200 pounds and 16 hands high
in the nearby stables

and the one assigned to you, *Johnnie*
— for nine months it was yours

For a long time, our mother kept those letters
stowed them away in a shoe box
on a top shelf in her bedroom closet

Whatever happened to them I don't know
maybe the fragmentary memories are a boy's
exaggeration of that time and place
yet I am so clearly there in a prairie dream
and spy you riding tall and straight
and proud into that lush savanna
with its never-ending sweep

Moon Dancing in Stillness

Checking the calendar: full moon
    quarter moon
        new moon

Checking out the birthdays of my
children:

Elise: Jan. 15, full moon,
dazzling and bursting, contented to sit
and peer down
over scarred maples near her window

and she, satisfied to sit at an old
Royal typewriter
or to bend back the covers
of my favourite books

— the moon, yawning and bored at
such indifference

André: Sept 19, sliver of the moon
like a skate blade
turning on a frozen pond sheltered
and ringed by poplars

recall perching him on a snow bank
to rest while I cleared the ice
— this two-year-old yearning to skate
Later, my frozen fingers tying up his
skates

MARTY GERVAIS

Stéphane: Oct, 22, new moon,
its beautiful halo high
over the River Mian in Frankfurt
I run, carrying him over one shoulder
through windy rainy streets

Another moment: Stéphane digging
down into a corduroy pocket to pull out
broken lifesavers — joy at holding in
the flat of a tiny hand a constellation of quarter moons

Gabriel: Sept. 4. Sliver of the moon,
and this boy impatient in the car seat
furiously scratching away the frost
from the side window and shouts
how that moon in the night sky
was like a broken finger nail

Those perfect days
Full moon
   quarter moon
      new moon

moons dancing in stillness
before my children
   dancing
   dancing
   dancing

The Galaxy

You could never get a straight answer
out of Ron — he'd tell you the car
would be ready tomorrow
and tomorrow would come
and he'd say he had to order a part
and it would be ready Friday
and Friday would come and he'd say the part
they sent was the wrong one
It might now be Monday or Tuesday
before he'd get the part and maybe Wednesday
before he'd get'er done
After a while it seemed Ron
had the car more than we did
Times when he'd surprise us
— getting up on a frozen winter morning
there'd be our Austin Healey
new fallen snow on the hood
sitting pretty under the window
like a new bike left in the middle of the night
by some good father
eager to please his neglected children
That was Ron —
Ron with a smile as big as an Amway salesman
wrench in one hand, bottle of coke in the other
Times when I'd telephone, and his wife would answer
and turn away from the phone and yell to him
that it was me on the line and I could hear
cursing and the clangor of tools
and metal being slammed down

Finally Ron would pick up the phone
Friendly and all, *How're ya doin' Marty?*
So what's up? And I was always reticent
to incite him with a reply like, *What's up?*
You stupid ass. Where's my car?
But I'd just ask politely *Well, just wonderin' about my car?*
Why I kept going back I don't know
— he was the only one who fixed
those English sports cars
Best in the business
But rarely did we ever see the car
— days would stretch to weeks, to a month
One day I asked for a loaner
and without hesitation Ron ambled out back
to get his own car, and I could hear an engine
firing up, revving in short blasts, followed suddenly
with billowing dust from around the side
gravel flying against the cement-block garage
The big Galaxy 500 approached
like the Marlboro man
with headlights as powerful as howitzers
It made me wonder why he gave me this
— the gas tank lay in the trunk, the lid flopped up
and down till we got some binder twine and anchored it
to the chrome bumper, and I wondered if I was driving
a Molotov cocktail instead of a Ford
That was fine — it was wheels, at least
until that morning when I sped along the highway
between Fergus and Guelph
and went to pass someone, my foot to the gas
the Galaxy V8 engine practically leaping
like a crazed hyena when suddenly the gas pedal
and all the linkage crashed through the floorboards

to the highway below
and I had to steer this beast to the edge, let it die
like an old work horse in the silence
of that summer morning —
As for the Austin, I must've poured a couple
of thousand into it till I owed so much
Ron had to sell it

I still wondered if he'd ever really fixed it
hadn't seen it for months when he asked
for the ownership to be signed over
and we agreed

After a while I lost touch
with Ron — it was like
losing a brother though

Much later, I got a postcard
that said he'd miscalculated
and I still owed
him $76.13

I never wrote back

Tell Me About Your Tomato Plants
When I Can't Sleep

For Donna

We might call it love —
this business of
telling each other
what really matters
what bothers us
on the worst days
what rankles us
and not so much
the petty things like
leaving off the top of
the toothpaste
or leaving behind
orange peels and
apple cores in the car
those things that
make us fume and swear
under our breath

At night when
it's time to sleep
and you curl up
I find that I cannot sleep
that I've carried the day
with me into this bed
and lie there
wide awake

That's when I need you
That's when I implore you
to tell me about your
tomato plants —

I yearn to drift
to think of nothing
more significant than
this, the puny tomato
plants that sprout in
our garden, that fruit
September brings
the most boring of
all fruits …
I then feel myself drift
drift in the soggy whisperings
you make of that
summer garden

To Be Now

For George and Irene Lee

He slipped his arms
around her waist
and took a stroll
along Woodward Ave.
past the vaudeville
theatres, the old boxing
clubs, the men and
women lolling about
in the cold
and she could feel
the wind whipping up
and around her legs
and she hooked
one arm around
his and held him close
and bent her head slightly
toward the chilly gusts
coming off the river
and he asked if she wanted
to see the Red Wings
and she shrugged
Nothing else mattered
right now
except to be here
to be with him
to be here
to be now

And so they walked
to the Olympia
and she never complained —
her new high-heels
clicking on the pavement
and he talked about
the season the Wings
were having, those
big farm boys with
hands as large as snow shovels
and she pretended
to be interested
but really all she
thought about
were the high heels
she'd ordered out
of the catalogue
and the day
they arrived —
her hands trembling
with excitement
how she held the
shoes like delicate birds
in her hands
and how the winter sun
poured through
the parlour window
and she imagined
walking with him —
this tall sheep farmer
whose manner was
gentle, whose promises
were true, and now

MARTY GERVAIS

there she was strolling
with him — their
honeymoon in Detroit
nothing else mattered
right now
except to be here
to be with him
to be here
to be now

Porch Spiders

For Calder

For weeks I have studied them —
at dusk they commence their work
— spinneret magic
fashioning an intricate silken gallery of traps
for their prey

in this night of waiting

first the safety line
then a web of sticky silk
that snags and snares
these bold intruders

I watch these wily orb-weavers
in a night of waiting
feel their patience tested
through a sleepy night
as they doze in silence
dreaming of feasting on everything
that nudges their invisible wall

No escaping in this night of waiting

They sense the vibrations of an interloper
a trespasser having blundered blindly
into its neighbourhood —

In an instant, they leap lightly
through the radial scaffolding
eight eyes, eight legs, sharp fangs
racing for the kill

I wait for these wily orb-weavers
to spin their victims
dress them for death
and wrap them tightly in fine silk

No escaping in this night of waiting

Dinner is served

Seeing the Dead at Gettysburg

Alexander Gardner and Mathew Brady photographing the Civil War

The photographers rode in, long after
they had already started burying the dead
landing upon the carnage with
their buckboard darkrooms and cumbersome
view cameras and tripods, and they stormed
into the smoke and stench, shooing away
hundreds of vexatious black vultures
that swarmed upon carrion mounds of dead horses

and maybe these picture-takers saw themselves
as no better, as they, too, scavenged
the still bodies of the dead
desperate for suitable subjects to tell the story
of this war, but dutifully fanned out to catch
the right light, the perfect angle of the sun

but the dead weren't always cooperative
— sometimes it meant moving the corpses
especially when they failed to die
in the right spot, often a better vantage
over there and *not here*, and so taking the pictures
meant lifting and dragging and hauling
the gory cadavers across an open battlefield
to reposition them so they lay posed
and properly draped in the foreground
for the cameramen — torn tunics bloodied
and slightly askew, and trusty
.58 caliber Springfields nearby .

all the while gray smoke drifted and ascended
and fell back in among the dead accentuating
a sullen background where one might make out
a soldier stirring in the hazy distance
riding a horse in the aftermath of a battle

It didn't matter if this staging was all a lie —
as for the dead they found it hard
to put on a good face

Moments Before the Old Presses Started at the *Windsor Star*

The first thing you'd see were
the hands, gloved and ink-stained
then the faces of men dwarfed by
the three-storied leviathan that sprawled out
in the morning ready to rouse and rise
You'd eye the pressmen pacing the perimeter
of this giant and see them stretch long clean sheets
of paper from giant rolls through its idle frame

They knew the monster well and knew
to wait and knew to hear its glory

I used to slide down from the newsroom
to stand nearby and watch, and hear the voices
over the faint growl of this prodigious creature
I'd see them carrying heavy metal plates
clamping them into place, and watching them fit
the curved cylinders to its pulsating contours
catch the slow mumble among
the men as they moved to feed the beast
to make it come alive, to make it stir

They knew the monster well and knew
to wait and knew to hear its glory

These were the men clambering at dawn
among tiered platforms and galleries
built around this slumbering creature
the first to spot the headlines
to read the world upside down and backwards

They knew the monster well and knew
to wait and knew to hear its glory

First Letter to Martin de Porres from Lima

I've tried to figure out what surprised me most in finding you here
... Swinging from the rear-view mirror of this cab is a cloth scap-
ular ... Mulatto saint among the poor ... Cabbie says you're also
the patron of stolen hubcaps, pilfered keys, ignition troubles ...
One night two thugs and a woman huddled in the back seat of his
VW, a pistol jammed to his head, ordered him to hand over the
keys ... But the hijackers failed to get the cab started ... Flooded
the engine ... Finally fled into the streets ... Cabbie shouting after
them to throw him the keys ... By the time he recovered the keys
on the darkened Lima streets, the car was no trouble to get going
and the cabbie got down on the pavement and thanked you for
this miracle ... Is this what surprised me? To hear this straight
from my childhood when I took your name? That I'd be sitting in
the back of this battered cab hearing about you ... Take away the
habit, change the hairstyle and you'd be Michael Jackson ... But
here your feet slide in the shadows beneath eyes and hands that
yearn for more than words.

Lima, Peru

Letter to an old woman on the road into the Andes

At first I thought I was an intruder, but the priest said it was fine, and your family nodded approval for me to step into the dark bedroom of your house ... Your face bewildered, expectant ... He held you and prayed with you ... Told me it was OK to take photos ... Even shifted the family away from the only window to let in more light ... A daughter, in fact, wanted a picture taken with you ... Stood silently beside the bed ... The priest anointed you, giving earthly farewell, making the sign of the cross, cutting the ribbon to the afterlife, and you slipped smoothly into the afternoon light above this tiny village that clings to the road like a young child to its mother — a town that flags down the Catholic priest on his weekly sojourns to the missions ... The priest is a local politician, someone to hate, to love, to use ... The priest bids goodbye, shakes hands with everyone, climbs back into the truck ... From the back room of the house, I imagine someone slipping a sheet over your face

Zana, Peru

He Couldn't Fix the Tractor

I take the highway
that runs past the tiny house
near the gas pumps
I mouth a silent prayer
for my mother who told us
about summer evenings
when her uncle the faith
healer stopped by
the Studebaker turning into
the drive. his neatly-cut
pants. the jacket, the lapel
bursting with a rose
his smile broad and the
hands, the slim delicate hands
of a man of prayer scrubbed
white and pink, the hands
that brought him money
and fame, the hands
that brought hope to
French families in the flat
lands of Essex County
My mother told me
he used to bound in through
the side door, bearing gifts
his eyes blue and penetrating
as they drank in the scene
in the big kitchen where
the men gathered at noon
tired from chores
and her uncle would start

talking, the words that
would make the men forget
the fields, the work outside
forget the mortgage, the broken
down tractor and the hired
hand who waited by the
cement silo, waited for
the others to come
and my uncle would talk and
talk and talk, words of
hope, of God, and Christ
and the Holy Ghost
of Satan and Evil
of the broken down tractor
as a sign of a contract broken
with the land, with God
and now it was time to atone
and the men would listen to him
reaching as they did for
a pipe or chewing tobacco
as the afternoon turned
grey and cold, as his words
turned their thoughts
back upon themselves
and then he'd stride out
to the Studebaker parked
in the yard under the elms
and he'd still be talking
and that's when my mom
asked if he could fix the tractor
that stood still in the field
like a stubborn mule that
wouldn't move, and he knelt

down beside her
— she, being all of six years old
— and he said, "Honey
I can fix bones and muscles.
I can fix fevers and gout.
I can fix bad eyes and twisted limbs
… But I don't know a damn thing
about tractors — that's for
someone else … Man made
them!" And with that
her uncle swung open the
large shiny door of his
Studebaker, and wished them well
and said he's pray for the tractor
… That's about all …
I think of him and my mom
that day in the summer, maybe
it was 1924 … Imagine
her standing on the bottom
step of that porch at the side
and her uncle's big car
sprawling in the summer sun
and the hands that couldn't
get the tractor started

The Hands: Muhammad Ali

The hands I noticed first —
I sat down across from him
knowing the swagger
and bluster and swiftness
and now before me
he moved with aching slowness
not with the grace of history

still, his words were in perfect timing
slow, yet ever calculating
not surprising — they always were that way

still, it was always the mouth that worked the room
with hands following in rabbit jabs
— a flash and blur of fists punching
the air, punctuating the poetry

That day there was none of that —
his words sadly emptied into silence
— hands moved in a mime of slow motion

or so I thought —
when all at once he took me by surprise
his left hand suddenly soared and swiped
the air above my head

I felt myself ducking

but it was his mouth that championed
the moment — as it always did
— that self-satisfied beaming smile
breaking across his handsome mug

Meeting Thoreau at the Gas Station Diner

I gave up trying to get a ride and leaned up
against a Red Maple well off the road and fell
asleep though intermittent passing cars turning
on that bend showered me with their lights
and in the morning I crossed over to
a gas station, borrowed the key to a dimly-lit
bathroom at the back of the building
and washed my face and arms and stared
at myself in a cracked mirror wondering
what I was doing, and why it didn't matter
— the sink was black with axle grease and
the lopsided toilet seat was split in two
Then I headed to the station's diner for coffee
settling on a stool at the counter, ordered toast
all I could afford, and opened
Walden: A Life in the Woods
to read: *I leave the towns behind and am lost in*
some boundless heath, and life becomes gradually
more tolerable, if not even glorious
A man sitting nearby asked what
I was reading, and I told him it was Thoreau's classic
and he nodded like it was familiar, then picked up
his coffee mug and moved over to a seat
next to mine and said, *We need only travel enough*
to give our intellects an airing ... Again Thoreau
Word for word from the book, from memory
and so the talk went, and soon the waitress
brought over a large china plate of eggs and ham
and potatoes, courtesy of the man next to me
and he smiled, then stood up, and departed
and I watched him wending his way past parked cars
in the gas station lot before taking a path
beyond the highway and vanish into the woods

Jimmy Sleeps Alone

I saw him once at the *Mercury Bar* in Detroit
— there he was, mouth running off and
arms and hands waving all about
above a fat burger on a plate

and it surprised me that he only ever drank soda
and never smoked and there he was after
a Tigers game, sitting alone, chatting up
a waiter, and I couldn't believe my eyes

— there he was the Teamster boss yammering
in his last days in Detroit, and later I read
how the day he went missing he telephoned
his wife Josephine from a payphone

how he'd been stood up at a lunch meeting
how two mobsters dumped him
into a 55-gallon drum, and loaded it
onto a truck and drove him to New Jersey

Others claim he's buried beneath the RenCen
and for years, Detroiters trekked to a local bakery
to scoop up "Jimmy Hoffa cupcakes" decorated
with a zombie hand sticking out of the icing

No matter what, Detroiters keep digging for him
in backyards, under foundations, new building sites
but *Jimmy sleeps alone*, and I know for a while
after his sudden disappearance, I struggled

to recall what he'd been mumbling at the *Mercury*
and swear I never killed Jimmy Hoffa, and I swear
he isn't buried in my backyard in Windsor —
the city dug up the sewer lines last spring

Reading Glasses

My wife keeps losing
her reading glasses
Buys them by the dozen
knowing if she has misplaced them
they'll be in any one
of a dozen places — the car
kitchen countertop
bathroom commode
near the phone
on the patio table
in any one of four
or five purses
maybe in a winter coat
maybe in the pocket
of a blazer
My wife keeps losing
her reading glasses
and doesn't seem to worry
— they'll turn up
yet she keeps searching for them
usually clutching in one hand
the thing she needs to read
those few lines of a note
left out for her
maybe a telephone number
or recipe or bank statement
My wife keeps losing
her reading glasses
She drives to Zellers
finds a prescription

that fits her eyes
and strolls out in
the afternoon sunlight
with the new pair
tucked away in a purse
in a place she's certain
to find them the next time
she picks up a book
My wife keeps losing
her reading glasses
I can't help but watch her
as she frantically
searches for them
when she's handed a menu
I can't help but imagine
a dozen pairs
folded up and asleep
like tiny quiet birds
awaiting her call

The Motel on Main Street

I was nearly 12, and wandered
by the u-shaped motel
that sat on the main drag
like an old aunt refusing to bid goodbye

I was taking a shortcut through the parking lot
making my way to a friend's
when I noticed a door ajar
in one of the units —

a sudden blur in the gloom of that room
a single light partly silhouetting a woman
slipping on a summer dress
over her head and down over bra and panties
hands smoothing out the cotton
momentarily looking up, spotting me
standing stock still in the lot
I want to think she just smiled and turned
escaping into darkness of the room
I continued my way to my friend's
but never forgot that instant —

Tonight, now 73 years old, I shuffle
into the cramped motel office
check in, ask for Room 106
and the hotel keeper hands me the key

I sit on the edge of the bed
coat and hat still on, slumped before a mirror
Why am I here? Maybe it's to gather
that moment into a bouquet
of darkness, of light, of beauty
something fraught and forsaken
and suddenly she is there —

or is that simply a mere gesture
of trailing light from a passing car

yet she is here, sitting beside me
leaning over to slip on her shoes
saying goodbye, summers long past
all of her now in a silhouette
brightening into a whisper of light

Three-year-old Granddaughter on a Summer Dock

for Vivi

You dance in summer sunlight
a little girl wearing a sparkly tutu on a wooden dock
in a lake so dark and blue
and I wonder why it is I have not written
and wonder about your journey across an ocean
and wonder about the words
that soar about you so unfamiliar
You stand in a summer now
a little girl whose gestures light up the day
and I wonder what it is about you
that has kept me so silent
Maybe it's the words I cannot find
Maybe it's the summer long past that reminds me
I cannot hold on to such shimmering moments
as you pirouette and praise the summer warmth
I see you silhouetted on a sunlit dock
in a lake so dark and blue
a little girl sashaying in a sparkly tutu
and see you whirl in a moment so pure and silent
yet still hear the forest all around clamour and commend
your playful moment till the sky melts into stillness
into a lake so dark and blue

What You Don't See in Pictures

The photograph of Brig. Gen. Nguyen Ngoc Loan
of South Vietnam's National Police
shooting Viet Cong officer Nguyen Van Lem

His hands were bound behind his back
and he wore a plaid shirt, two buttons
undone and open wide at the neck
and a touch of wind played and flipped
back the bottom of his untucked shirt

or maybe it's the way his body twisted
abruptly as the man next to him —
a thin man with a receding hairline
in a bulky flak-vest — fired a bullet
from a snub-nosed .38 sidearm pistol
into his right temple

That is the picture you see —
the iconic Vietnam photograph
by Eddie Adams

a 1/500th of a second snapshot
freezing that look on the man's face
a fat lip, shocked grimace, eyes shut
and tousled hair

and a bullet crashing
through his brain at 600 mph

and the recoiled pistol
slightly upturned in the hand
of the soldier delivers
the crowning statement

all this in a single 35 mm frame

and some claim if you look closely
you can make out the bullet
in the hot haze of that first day
of February 1968 in Saigon

Yet it's the picture seconds later
you never see — the thin man with the pistol
slipping it back into his holster as casual
as tucking away a wallet after making a purchase

or the man in the plaid shirt, slumped
in a pool of blood on the pavement
like a curled-up safari kill
skinny legs and bare feet

It's the picture you never see
the man with the pistol years later
sleeves rolled up to the elbows
just like that day in February heat of Saigon
now smiling and leaning
at a lunch counter in the pizzeria
he opened near Washington D.C.

But pictures tell only *half-truths*
says Eddie Adams — they never
tell the whole story

Obits

Every morning I scoop up the paper
from between the doors of my house
spread the pages out on the kitchen table
a steaming mug of tea beside
and check out each one of the obits
scan the names to see if I recognize anybody

This isn't something that comes with old age
or fear of missing out about old friends
passing away and never sending flowers
— I've always done this, a practice from
my days as a reporter, the first impulse
in the morning, reading through the obits

then telephoning funeral homes to find
if anyone of public prominence had died
and from there we'd collect details —
family phone numbers, dig through the "morgue"
the name we gave to our archives
and bit by bit type out a story for the editor

The practice has now turned to imagining —
piecing together another story, finding a twist
of plots with dialogue and mystery and irony
wondering which of the children or grandchildren
will take over the company, run for political office
or wind up embezzling the family fortune

Second Letter to D

So what has happened? Riding home in this old Chev. Billowy snowy Saturday. Reading Ginsberg aloud ... Later, stocking feet wet from snow. Reciting old fifties poems ... It's great to hear them again, you said. Sunny afternoons 16 years ago when I read aloud to you ... Now you're off at the store and I address them to two-year-old Stéphane as he rushes about the living room with a hockey stick ... The great Sunflower Sutra ... His golden head bobbing among furniture and books, chanting along ... The Kaddish poems ... and Stéphane flashes a smile from the other room ... eating words alive, devouring rhythms ... The purest product of the future emerging in each stride ... Later, he lies on his back and I change his diaper, read him *The Fall of America*, the extravaganza of the protest years ... Dylan, Peter Paul and Mary or what you called the soft prayers of the air waves ... Stéphane somehow gleans the brightness of those lines as they drift about him ... Our lives having flowed into his tiniest soul ... The afternoons, conversations, books, apartments, the sameness of everything we clung to ... We glimpse it this Saturday afternoon sensing something lost of quiet idealism ... Now, I fold diapers and miniature undershirts and Stéphane sleeps beyond the radio jazz this Saturday afternoon and I hum Ginsberg's mantra verses so they might stir him, so they might fill him with the peace I feel this cold day ... The glare of the snow through the window keeps me alive to it all ... Finished the laundry, and cut a piece of birthday cake from Kresge's ... A trumpet wails out an echo to the Plutonian Odes and Stéphane, sensing its meaning, shifts among bedclothes in a faraway room ...

Summer in Detroit

A flimsy wooden seat
from Detroit's old Olympia
bought for $25
is the closest thing I have
to the Beatles
who once played in that arena
in 1964, and again in 1966

and I think of my friend
who remembered it was nearly midnight
when the Beatles' Greyhound pulled away
from the Olympia —

he could hear Fab Four singing *Long Tall Sally*
as teenage girls rushed into the street
to trail after the bus —
Cleveland bound, an all-nighter

Someone said they heard their laughter
spotted them wave from the open windows
a humid August night
swore they tossed their cufflinks
to frantic stretched out hands

My 18-year-old high school buddy
had skipped class that day
to hang out at the Whittier Hotel downtown
and dialed all day long a radio station
so he could win one square inch
of the sheets Lennon slept on

I don't know if any of it is true
I don't care — the broken down
seat from the Olympia rests
in a corner of my basement

I'm struggling to find some kind of metaphor
for how I should feel, some lyric moment
for this brush with greatness
as I sit down on that wooden chair
the hum of the furnace
in the silence of a summer afternoon

but this is nothing to compare
with the postage stamp-sized remnant
from John Lennon's bed
that rests in a dresser drawer
in an envelope from the radio station

I swear I can hear someone sleeping

The Wedding Dress

The first time I saw it
I was six
and sunlight spilled
through the bedroom window

I lifted this limp white satiny dress
from a flattened cardboard box
in the cedar chest
I raised it high above my head
— the fitted narrow waist
with a row of fabric-covered buttons
and the invisible side buttons
along the left side seam
I could hear Arthur Godfrey on the radio
in the other room
the kettle's whistle
I could hear the man next door
working on the roof of his house

I held the dress high above me
fingers marveling at its smoothness
lost in its whiteness
its full length skirt
cascading gracefully
in alternating tiers of sheer chiffon

when suddenly my mother's voice
at the doorway told me
it was a summer day like this
it was at the farm in Stoney Point
when she first put on the dress

and how she had gone upstairs
in the room shaded by the front yard maple
and how she remembered
gleaming cars zigzagged in the yard
and her fingers fidgeting
as she slipped on this dress

how the day was hot and cloudless
and how her father complained
there hadn't been enough rain

and she told me she had waited
forever resting on the edge of the bed
for her mother to come and approve

how she sat there
staring out the window
shoes resting beneath her
like two sleeping doves
on the hardwood floor

then she heard her mother's
voice at the edge of the room
the softness of the words
enveloping her in that moment

and she knew it was time
to take the car to the church
its steeple towering above the flatness
of the farm fields
and she wondered then
if it was all a mistake

Backyard Workshop

It was always after supper and always
in the summer and always after
my father had had a couple of beers
and read *The Windsor Daily Star*
that he'd gesture for me to join him
for a ride over to George Avenue

to visit my grandfather and I'd scramble up
onto the patterned broadcloth seats
of the big Chevrolet
I was six or seven then
and we'd make our way along the river
and down George to the two-story house

and I'd sprint from the car and race
through the garden to find my grandfather
in the cramped little shed, the painful whine
of the table saw and him leaning over his work
sleeves rolled up cleanly past the elbows
spectacles nearly slipping off his nose

and he'd turn to us with a broad smile
in a world of saws and chisels and stacks
of boards and a floor covered in wood shavings
and a dangling bare lightbulb above
affording him that last wink of light
at the end of a summer day

and it was there I'd watch and eavesdrop
as he spoke a language I'd never learn
a lexicon I'd never comprehend, words
tumbling out of him as he unraveled
the mysteries of a half-blind dovetail joint
the science of making a perfect doweling

Believe me, it was easier to understand
the Blessed Trinity but here I'd watch
transfixed by these puzzling words, lost
in their rhythmic sounds, and still patiently
marvel at all these pieces coming together
while I surrendered to disbelief, seeing

my grandfather moving with the grace
of an artist yet bringing to life something
as simple and ordinary as a kitchen cabinet
with recessed drawer fronts and doors
and I remember nothing of the how-to
the choice of tools he used or why —

nothing but the steadied refrains
of hammers and saws amid the melodious
and mysterious turns in his voice as he spun
unfathomable secrets before me — it was all
poetry, alive and mesmerizing in summers
at dusk in the workshop behind his house

Room With a Face

For Howard and Jeanette Aster at La Roche D'Hys, France

The room glows
from a storybook quarter moon
that hovers in the window
and the ghost-white cows far below
doze away in the valley
dreaming of tomorrow's
sunshine

and I fall to sleep
seeing the moon
press its face to the glass
wishing it might join me
in this night of stories

I tell it instead to stay where it is
I tell it to wait and see
I tell it to sing me a lullaby
as I wait to fall away free

The room glows
from a storybook quarter moon
I touch its grimacing face
I feel it depart — graceful
and splendid —
soaring into darkness
so the meadow can bloom full of light

I wish myself to sleep
hearing the moon breathe
and I sail with it safely into the night sky
the drifting clouds beneath

The room glows
from a storybook quarter moon
and I feel myself lifting into darkness —
my limbs soaring among stars
and glimpsing the house
and slumbering cows
in the sleepy meadow below

I tell the moon to whisper its rumours
I tell it to linger and hear
I tell it to sing of its passage
into a place without fear

The Cure

I was not quite five years old
and I stepped out onto Ouellette Avenue
trailing my father, my tiny hands shading
my eyes from the dazzling sun
after my very first eye exam

I started wearing glasses two days later
and they rested unnaturally on my nose
like a sparrow dreaming of flying off
somewhere soon —

what followed were years
of schoolyard fights and cracked lenses
snapped temples, broken bridges, missing screws
and my father's warnings he'd let me go blind
if I didn't care for them any better

But my brother cooked up a cure
in a comic book from the bodybuilder
Charles Atlas, the man who claimed
to rip up a New York phone book in half
bend an iron rod into a horseshoe shape
with his bare hands, and now boasted
of curing blindness with well water

and so my brother offered to lower me
upside down and slowly into the well
at my grandfather's farm near Stoney Point
and there I'd slip into the cold deep expanse
wearing only a bathing suit, and open my eyes wide
underwater for a minute and a half
— and that's all there was to it

I was terrified — I was five
and my head was swimming in doubts
fearing the rope might snap
or my brother might lose his grip
besides, I couldn't swim, and I'd never get out

and so instead he calmly led me to the farmyard
to the well near the chicken coop
and pumped the handle till water gushed
and he filled a rounded and wide tin pan
that rested on the ground and told me
to take in a deep deep breath, dip my face
eyes open wide, into the water
and he'd count down the time
for the cure to happen

but he kept pushing my head down
my eyes staring into the scratched surface
of the basin, then finally lifted my face
from the frigid well water, and I scanned
the farmyard, saw the red blur of the hen house
and a zigzagging clothesline wavering
in the windy yard, and my dad's car
near the wooden steps of the farmhouse

and my brother clowning about nearby
laughing his head off —

I'd wear glasses for the rest of my life

Tomato Wine

For Al Purdy

I drove all one late afternoon back home
from Ameliasburgh, bottles of tomato wine
clinking in the cardboard boxes
in the trunk of my car

a toddler crying in the back seat, a young
daughter daydreaming, and my wife and I
fishtailing the back roads that hot summer day
hauling the tomato wine that Al made

and made us take with us when we left
his A-frame on Roblin Lake, even though
I swore there was no room, but he found
a way to wedge the boxes into the car

and so I carried the bottles back to our place
and stored them in the basement and
they stayed there, year after year, never
uncorked or tried, and though I grumbled

I wouldn't throw them out, in fact, when
we moved, the cardboard boxes and
two dozen bottles of tomato wine made their way
with everything else, and once again

they were stored in my basement and stayed
there for years, sometimes being shuffled
from one corner to another, and never once
were opened, till finally one day in a moment

of clarity, or reckless abandon, whatever
I gathered up the broken cardboard boxes
of tomato wine and placed them gently in the backseat
of my car and drove them to the dump

and couldn't help but duck down as I sped away
somehow suspecting to find Al, shirtsleeves rolled
tightly up to the elbows and cursing up a storm for
how we had just wasted a good batch of homemade wine

Belonging Somewhere: Rosa Parks

I noticed her —
sitting in a corner waiting for Mother Teresa
waiting for this saint to make her way
down those wooden steps
and leave behind the hallelujahs

to embrace Detroit's Cass Corridor,
soup kitchens, single mothers, the homeless

I went over, and she smiled
and after a few moments nodded tiredly
to the same story she's told
a million times before.
all about that commute home after
working all day as a seamstress
and settling into a seat
in the colored section of
that Montgomery Alabama bus
and refusing to give it up
to a white man

It was the winter of 1955
and there was nothing that was going
to budge Rosa from that comfortable seat

Now she rested beside me on a wooden chair
in the basement of this church —
hands folded over her knees
happy at escaping all the formal liturgy
from the sanctuary above

not the least bit impatient to meet Mother Teresa

The bus story finished abruptly
and Rosa waved a hand for me to let it rest —
she's told it so many times before
so I changed the topic
·*How about them Tigers?*

and her face brightened, and she muffled a giggle
and soon the focus was the neighborhood
— the mission Mother Teresa was starting

Her battles will never end it seems
— they've been a part of her fabric growing up
memories in the south of a grandfather
pacing in front of their house with a shotgun
as the Ku Klux Klan marched by

nightmares still of a white man next door
trying to rape her and in all the wildness
she was thinking *If he wanted to kill me
and rape a dead body, he was welcome
but he'd have to kill me first*

activism in seeking justice for black victims
of white brutality and sexual violence
openly calling Malcolm X her personal hero

but I didn't see this in this quiet woman
seated in a church basement
amid a broken-down landscape of crack houses
and burned-out shells of buildings

I saw uncertainty over what
she was going to tell Mother Teresa
because no one else knew the neighborhood
knew the people by name
knew their struggles

yet everybody knew her

As I got up to leave, Rosa looked up
and I saw it still there in her eyes
— all that fire and tenacity
simmering and alive

yet the truth was in her own words
about the loneliness of being a rebel

I am nothing. I belong nowhere

Nude Bride

I leave the nude bride
She is asleep
Leave her
a clock on the mantel
a drawing
dishes to do

Hips

Like the curve
of a hockey stick
the soft bend in the road
at dusk, the way
a branch bows
with the full weight
of apples in the fall
I saw curves everywhere —
I thought of all
the young girls whose
figures would blossom
with my adolescent
fantasies, their hips
swaying in the cool spring
the slope of the jeans
or the gingham dress
the way they moved
with unctuous grace
When I was 12
the deciding factor
my buddy told me
was a good set of hips
— the pick of a good
wife lay with the hips
perfect for childbearing
and we'd stand
on the street
at the Parkview Diner
and take inventory
of the young moms

size up their hips
cock our head
to one side
and nod in agreement
over the perfect set —
one as slender and lithe
as a balsam tree, others
as wide and proud
as the bumper
of a Chev Impala
I had become
sexually aware at 12
silently measuring
the half-moon like
curves as they sauntered
down aisles, as they moved
between tables in the
school cafeteria
I saw curves
everywhere —
catching the Yankee
Billy Martin sliding
to one side to make
a play at second
his hips in the October
series like the elegance
of a cougar moving
to snare his prey
I saw hospital
pinstripers pouring
out at the end of a day
their lovely bodies
as smooth as a warm

current in the lake
I saw Elvis bump
and grind, his white
suedes flashing on
a darkly-lit stage
hips swiveling
like a well-oiled engine
I saw curves everywhere —
I didn't see breasts
I didn't fixate
on crotches
or the slope of
a neckline
or the nakedness
of thighs
I saw hips
I saw hips
I saw hips

Driving to Dresdon

For Donna

You sleep beside me
in the car as we make
our way through wintry
darkness to a Friday
night arena
to see our son play hockey
We wind our way in
darkness, the fields
flat in the open, the
orange lights of barns
and houses spilling
onto the powdery
white lawns, the single
yard light near the barn
and a man walking
from a pickup
to a house,
and a woman
standing with the
door slightly ajar
calling him
and he's saying
nothing, just coming
toward the house
and their lives
lift in me, make
me wonder about us
the reasons we
say things that

hurt or say things
that make us believe
in love again
You sleep now
as we make
our way silently
through the snowy
night to this arena
in the cold light of
a moon to watch
a son who might raise
his head a moment
before a face off
to see if we're there
in that Friday night
arena, to see if
we dream
as he does
for that perfect
moment when he
finally moves like the
promise of spring

Lucky Days

For Stéphane

My son collects chestnuts
to tuck into his hockey bag
for good luck

I told him
Hemingway rolled them
in his hands in his tweed pockets
every morning before he wrote
believing the work
would go better

Today in this arena
in the Alsace region
the late afternoon glow
floods the ice
through this wall of windows
and the chestnut trees
step forward to press
their eager faces against
the cold glass
to catch sight of the boy
who claims
he needs no luck

Things That Counted

There were only a few things you had to keep clear in those days —
*Who had the highest batting average? Who had the lowest ERA? Who
won the Stanley Cup last year?* I had little trouble with any of these,
but year after year the nuns stumped me with the first question in
the Baltimore Catechism: *Who is God?* My brother Billy pulled me
aside one day and told me not to worry — the truth was, he said, I
don't think they know either — that's why they keep asking.

Leaving My Sins Behind

It was the same every Saturday afternoon when I was eight — my mother dispatching us to the matinees with only enough for a ticket, along with a warning to return home only once we'd stopped by the church and gone to confession ... Billy and I would race from the movies to Our Lady of Guadeloupe, file into line, tell Father Mooney how we'd lied, disobeyed our parents, cheated on tests, and entertained bad thoughts ...

One Saturday — desperate to go off to the bathroom — I decided to wait it out in line for fear of losing my place ... And even after pushing past the curtain I had to wait for Billy on the other side to spew out his sins — probably much the same as mine ...

Finally, my turn, and Father Mooney slid open the panel. In darkness I started: "Bless me Father, for I have ..." but couldn't hold it anymore ... feeling that sudden uncontrollable generous warm wet rush into my cotton pants ... I started over, sobbing: "Bless me, Father for I have just peed in your confessional ..." The kindly bald-headed priest, straining to make sense of my desperation, asked gravely, "How many times have you done this, my son?" As if I would make a practice out of it ... In frustration — trying to stem the flow and save face — I blurted out, "I'm doing it right now, Father!" Then fled the confessional box, holding myself, and scurrying home, worried sick over how big a sin this was, how terrible the penance might be, how many novenas, stations of the cross, indulgences, rosaries, pilgrimages it would take for final redemption.

The Cow in Your Kitchen

for John B. Lee in Brantford, Ontario

I shuffle back to my room
along tunnel-like hospital corridors
I've been up since 4 a.m.
reading the *Sunday Times*
It's now 5:30
Soon the sun will loom through
the east window slatted with blinds
and nurses will rest a tin bowl
of soapy water on the chair
in the corner where I can wash up
Now I want to sleep
I fall headlong into a dream
— sleeping pills and
Gravol finally kicking in
I see this cow in your kitchen
with Carnation Cream cow eyes
blinking at me with big
girlish lashes, and it won't
budge and I call out
but you are in the other
room talking on the phone
The cow shifts its clumsy heaviness
and nudges me against a table
I'm thinking why the hell
is there a cow in your kitchen
and what's your family
thinking by having it loll
and laze on the linoleum floor?
Now the cow leans and groans

It's tired and wants to lie down
on the table beside the flowers
I brought you yesterday
It peers up at the clock over
the stove and knows it's time
for its afternoon nap
and bellows out one more moo
before nodding off
The cow is in my way
You don't seem to care
It's part of the family
like a loveable old dog or cat
I watch its big eyes flutter
then finally shut
Now it's dreaming —
maybe going on family picnics
riding in the back of
the truck like an offish kid
with big lips, funny ears
and a weight problem
maybe riding the school bus
getting weird looks
maybe staying up late
with Mom and Dad
watching Planet of the Apes
I sleep and I dream
of your cow and its dream
as it muses over its happy
contented life in Brantford, Ont.
where it's not uncommon
to have a cow as a family pet

Lazy Eye

Don't call it lazy
— it's simply not paying attention
It's looking to the left
when the other's peering to the right
It's looking at the ceiling
when the other's studying my shoes
It's spying a woman
turning the corner
her red hair grazing her slim shoulders
notices her bright blue shoes
the A-line dress
Meanwhile the other eye
spots a headline in the paper
being read by a man in a nearby café
Lazy? No — Curious. Bold. Nosy.
It wanders like a happy thief
down a department store aisle
It wanders like a canoe set adrift
It wanders by itself
seeking wisdom or truth
the eye with a mind of its own

Summer Nights Outside
Metropolitan Hospital

For Rosemary

I saw my grandmother
in the back bedroom of her little house
She was dying of stomach cancer
I was 10 —
By summer she was
on the third floor of the hospital
I'd visit with my father
but my sister and I had to wait in the car
We'd roll on the backseat of a sprawling Plymouth
making ugly faces and laughing
or trying to guess which window was hers
We'd wait and wait until my father
would stroll out in the humid twilight air
with ice cream and ice-cold Vernors

After a while we didn't care
about my grandmother
We longed to be pampered
Every day begging our father
to take us to the hospital
We promised to wait by the curb
wait the hours out
for the treats

It all stopped when
my grandmother died

We missed the ice cream

Pavarotti at the Detroit Opera Theatre

Four years before the Grand Circus Park Theatre
reopened as the Detroit Opera House

You might've mistaken him for a fighter
with the World Wrestling Federation
this burly man so large, the full weight of him
moved in menacing confidence that late afternoon
as he paced outside beneath a sunny
blue downtown sky while another man with
a jangle of keys laboured away to unlock
a building practically collapsing upon itself

and once inside, the big man emerged
in the dusty gloom of the vast sweep of sagging
balconies and broken down theatre seats
and a ravaged and water-stained ceiling
but his eyes lit up when he spotted the stage

and rushed down an aisle, hopped over
mountains of toppled wooden beams
scrambled over shattered glass
and rounded the flooded orchestra pit
with a grand piano that floated like a turtle in the sun
and then he clambered onto the planked floor
arms now stretching out before him —
and the broad smile of his face now imagined
he stood before an audience
in Berlin, Vienna or Rome

MARTY GERVAIS

"I will sing here!" he told the other man
and waited not a minute as his thrilling voice
suddenly lit up and trumpeted into
every dark and diminished corner of the old theatre —
arms open in faith and the shining timbre
of Puccini's aria rousing and bringing
the place back to life once more

Guardian Angel

He's lazy and never around
when I need him
I drive down
to the coffee shop
in the early morning
and find him reading the paper
or talking to the locals

I want to tell him
he's not taking this seriously
— he's supposed to watch over me
He shrugs and says the rules
have changed
I can't reach him on Facebook
and he won't pick up his phone

I want to ask him how he got this job
Why me? Why him?
Luck of the draw, he shrugs
our birthdays, the same
and we both have bad eyes
a hearing problem
and can't eat spicy foods

But where was he in October 1950
the afternoon on Wyandotte
when I was four
and I ran between
two parked cars?
He was there, he says

coming out of the pool hall
to save me
to cup my bleeding head
on the warm pavement
to glare at the driver
who stood in the open door
of his Ford, worried sick
that I might die

He was there, he said
otherwise I might not
be having this conversation
and he was there again
when I lay curled up
and unconscious
in the hospital room one winter
swearing at the hospital staff
after bowel surgery
and he touched my lips
with his index and middle fingers
and quieted me

Besides, he's always there
and there's no point
having this conversation
— he's so far ahead
and knows so much more:
a hundred different languages
names of every star
in the universe, the physics
of flying
and the winner
of the Stanley Cup
every year till the
end of time

The History of My Clothes

I dress in the dark
so as not to wake my wife
when I get up at 5 a.m.
The pants
I wore yesterday
gabardines, blue,
34 in. waist, 30 in-seam
washable — bought
at Moore's on sale
Was $78, marked down 15%
now another 30%
for the summer sale
I'll wear them again
What about a shirt?
I won't turn on the lights
in the closet — I reach
out in blackness
like a blind man
and feel the lineup
on hangers, convinced
I can match the feel
of the fabric with the colour
I've mastered this
also memorized the order
from left to right:
three shirts in, I'll find
a blue broad cloth
button down, bought
at the Bay three years ago
15 neck, 34-35 sleeve
full price $43

Next to it are two silks
tailored in Hong Kong
very blousy
I won't wear them
too much like Mozart
whenever I extend my arms
loose-fitting sleeves drooping
and I feel the urge to play — notes
bouncing in my brain and imagine
I'm wearing one of those
courtly period powdered periwigs
I settle on a shirt
counted eight from the left
a *Daniel Hechter*, button down
cotton/polyester blend
robin's egg blue
I could be a stockbroker
— I'll take risks today
buy and sell immortal souls
like Lucifer, make a fortune
for some, ruin others
But first, I've got to find
some underwear — *Stanfields*
loose fitting, large
I hate anything gripping me
down there unless it's
of my own making
And my socks, black
always black — buy 10 pairs
at a time, all the same so
when they come out of the dryer
hot like croissants out of the oven
there's no worry over matching

Always the same price
three pairs, $9
cotton, stretchy
I'm ready now
I lay out the clothes on the bed
in the dark, my wife still
slumbering, first the *Stanfields*
now the socks, now the *Daniel*
Hechter and stand there a moment
feeling out of place
awkward like a hockey player
lounging about in full uniform
but without skates
Finally, the gabardines
I'm ready —
I feel like me
I am me
I'm everybody

The Hockey Equipment

I sat near the back step
of the apartment just
above the bank. and tried on
the equipment — shin pads
shoulder pads, elbow pads
The bank manager's wife
stood there watching me,
said I could have them
they had been her son's
she would just throw them
out if I didn't take them
I lugged the bag home
that night up main street
to my house, and dumped it out
on the basement floor
and tried it all on
again in silence, but for
the hum of the coal furnace
That winter I played my heart out
trying to make the travel team
and failed and wound up
playing early Saturday mornings
with boys as bad at hockey as I was
I remember noticing
the bank manager's wife showing up
a few mornings to watch
She just sat at one end of the arena
below the advertisement
for the dry goods store, same
spot a couple or three Saturdays

in a row, then I didn't see her again
All winter I wondered about why
she had come and I wondered about her son
and what happened to him
whether he ever made the hockey team
I couldn't remember his name, though
she must've told me, couldn't think
of what it was, and where was he anyway?
I was new to town and didn't know
the stories, the families, except for
my new friends, and maybe I scored
a half dozen goals, and by the end
of March I was packing away the
equipment in the basement
and thought of her son again
and finally asked a buddy of mine —
and he told me two winters before
I moved to town their son had fallen
through the ice on the south branch
of the river, playing hockey
had been on the travel team, a goal
scorer, hands like Jean Beliveau
and he was 15 and the Bears were looking
to sign him next season
The next winter when I opened the bag —
the embarrassment was overwhelming
of how badly I had played the winter
before, how the boy's mother sat there
those Saturday mornings in hope
of catching the grace and glory of
a son she no longer had

Boxcars in Swift Current

I scrambled up on a 20-ton boxcar
its tall doors open, and I sat down
on its wide flat wooden floor just about
the time the sun was going down
then felt the whole line of cars shift
and move and figured I was on my way
but in a matter of moments
I was riding off to a siding
to sit and watch the darkness collect
and a yardman walked past
and grinned but didn't say anything
and so all this romance of riding
windy boxcars across the prairie grassland
evaporated and I waited till the cars
finally stopped, and I jumped down
and made my way back to the yard
and saw the yardman making his way
toward me, smiling again, and now
shaking his head, and heard him ask
Where are you going? And I said I'd hoped
to make it to the coast, and he turned away
and with a wave of his left arm signaled for me
to follow, and I trailed after him to a pickup
and he opened the passenger door and told me
to get in, and he'd take me back
to the highway, and there was
no other choice — I'd have a better
chance hitching a ride there
And when he pulled over
to the shoulder of the Trans-Canada

he reached down and unlatched a tin lunch box
and pulled out a mickey, and offered it
and it burned all the way down
in my chest like the sun

The Outhouse

For Thomas Merton

The outhouse all by itself
on a rise just above the river
a few feet from the cabin
perched there like a sad broken down
car nobody wanted anymore

but it was a room with a view
with an opening of a tiny sliver of a moon
carved out in the cedar boards

and sitting in there you could watch
dawn break over the nearby bridge
and the town rouse in the milky darkness
and see a blanket of mist lift from the water

or you could study a wily spider leap
across its web in a high corner of planked
boards to feast on an intruder who will curse
the heavens for its unfortunate missteps

or be reminded of Thomas Merton
writing about the outhouse at the hermitage
at the Abbey of Gethsemani
and how each morning the monk would step
cautiously inside — wary eyes frantically searching
for 'king snake' and he'd address it formally
as if neither of them had any business being there

But here where I sat, I could spy the beginnings
of a day, feel it pull back the blankets
of the night, and move into the quiet rhythms
that define everything that we take on

and I wondered is this what the poet monk
was telling us when he said he marries
the silence of the forest and openly offers
to embrace its sweet dark warmth

Meeting the Dead in May

You will spend the day visiting the dead

— that's what my mother told me
when she buttoned up my stiff white shirt
and affixed a bow tie to the collar ...

I wore my brother's hand-me-down pants
and a pair of shiny black shoes.
I was dressed and ready for the dead.

I was probably five, and waited patiently
beside my father's Plymouth parked
under the lilacs in bloom
The weather was warm
and my buddy from across the street
ambled over and asked why
I was all dressed up

I told him I was going to meet the dead.

I had never seen a dead body before
except on television —
I was pretty excited

I was dressed and ready

My buddy told me he had seen
his dead uncle last winter — nothing special
He had expected his uncle's eyes
might be gaping, like the cattle-rustlers

on *Gunsmoke* when they lay
in the dusty street in Dodge City
dead at the hands of the righteous
Marshall Matt Dillon

I was dressed and ready
— eyes open or not

That day in early May I'd see two dead
when my father drove to Stoney Point
out to the farm near the lake
— the morticians had already been there
with embalming equipment

and at the first place we paused
in the parlor — cousins, and aunts
nodding in silence, barely a whisper when
suddenly a window blind let go and snapped up
and everyone abruptly turned to the deceased
as if they thought he might wake up

I made the sign of the cross —
I was dressed and ready for the dead

The second farm we stopped at
down by the Lighthouse belonged to the deceased —
no wife, no children, a bachelor farmer
and he lay in his coffin in the big kitchen
rosary beads twisted around his stubby fingers
I noticed his nails had been scrubbed clean

and everyone wore black, especially
a collection of gnarly old widows
who looked like witches — bony hands forever
reaching out to pinch my cheeks
and marveling at the color

I figured I'd be boiled alive with the apples

I was dressed and ready for the dead

Piano Hands

You have beautiful veins
the nurse told me
She unbuckled my left arm
and surveyed the stark
white landscape
of mapped highways
searching for a way in
a place to insert
the juncture for the IV
I had never thought
of myself like that
Why is it my mother
never told me this?
Instead I was praised
for having hands of a pianist
As a child, I'd study them
for hours wondering
why they couldn't play
I'd sit at the upright piano
in the living room
and command them
to play something
anything — jingle, exercise
birthday tune, anything
What do you know?
I'd ask, and my hands
would lie there
inert, disinterested, dumb
You have beautiful hands
my mother would say

— you'll play someday
you'll stand before throngs
and tell stories
with those hands
and at seven I'd sit
in front of our towering piano
and pretend
I'd sit up straight
I'd put on a bowtie
my first communion jacket
arrange the sheet music
and let my hands flutter over ivory
like seagulls dipping into the sea
up and down, sweeping over
the white white
my mind lost in the moment
a darkened concert hall
my beautiful hands
redefining grace
a crowd hanging on every note
Oh my beautiful hands
let them hear you
take us away
carry us into beauty

What Makes a Picture

Remembering George Lee

Two photographers, a poet and an old farmer
went in search of the jawbone of
the giant mastodon that had been unearthed
in 1890 on farm near Highgate — it was on loan
to the village's public library, and the farmer
hoped his visitors would see it, get a picture
before it was taken back to
its home in a North Dakota museum

and the farmer knew the farm where
it had been dug up, only a mile away
and knew the family, even recalled
some of the fuss about the skeleton
of this great beast, but the photographers
had made the trip to meet the farmer and his wife
and they rode up the lane way to where
the tall black barn stood on a hill

That's what lured the photographers —
the barn, the hill, the rolling landscape
around Highgate, this family, the vast sweep
of the land and the solitary sun above

They cared nothing for the mastodon

Yet the farmer insisted on pictures
of the creature's jawbone dug up among
tree roots and rocks in a nearby ditch —
forget the photos of him walking among

a mob of sheep or posing with his wife
at the gate, forget the crooked fence
or the silent sleeping tractors resting
in the shade of the barn

and so the photographers stepped out
into that summer day, and motored on down
into the village to snap pictures of the jawbone
of this great beast —

but went away puzzled over how
nobody mentioned the other creature unearthed
with the skeleton — the skull of a giant beaver
that had been the size of a black bear
with an eight-foot tail and teeth
the length of steak knives

Now, that would be a picture

Men at the Shell Station

It was late fall
and I would see the men at the back of
the Shell Station — a dim light of
the garage interior
the men resting on wooden milk crates
borrowed from the dairy
across the road — playing poker
a brand new '58 Monarch
on a hoist like a prize stallion
and me and my buddies outside
racing around the back to climb
atop a mound of discarded tires
and oil drums
to crouch at a broken window
and listen to the same old stories
mostly talk about women —
never their wives
mostly friends' wives
— horny little things
who couldn't control themselves
And we'd glance at one another
fearing our own mother's name
might be mentioned
but it never was
and we wouldn't have known
what to do if it was —
our brains stirring with secrets
imagining things
that made no sense to kids
barely 12, and after a while

our hands and feet were freezing
and we'd climb back down in darkness
and we'd stand in the street
and someone would light up
a crumpled cigarette
scrounged from some dad's ashtray
and take turns smoking it
and marvel at the rings
rising miraculously
in the cold fall air

Calling My Father

I came across
my father's old phone number
scrawled in the address book

— the numbers rolled off
so easily, the times
I called with
a piece of good news

or that moment
in late spring
when I telephoned
to tell my father
his son, my brother
was dying and
we had better
get down to the hospital

or the call I made
from Vancouver
when I was 20
and needed train fare
to return home
and heard
impatience
in my father's
gravelly voice

I sat and stared
at the number
for a long time
then dialed
letting it ring and ring
wondering if
I should hang up
if suddenly
a stranger answered

Deep down
I innocently hoped
someone
might pick it up
in Heaven

The Affairs of Death

About an hour after
my mother died
I was on my hands and knees
in the hospital room
scanning the tiled floor
for one of her tiny pearl earrings
— a small boy again
in her bedroom
on Prado Place, that
humid summer of 1950
wanting her attention
and kneeling there on the floor
beside her bed
yellow blinds pulled down
my mother yearning to sleep
I can't wake her
I can't wake her
but will she stop sleeping?

There I was that morning
just past dawn, sun barely
wiping away the sleep in its eyes.
my mother's face
far from dreaming
far from all of us now
seeing all that we can't see,
all that we fear

I envy that small boy
wanting her attention

I can't wake her
I can't wake her

June 12, 1992

Vladimir Horowitz: The American Tour Resumes in Detroit After the Death of His Mother

He was a boy when his mother slid in beside him
at the piano in the parlor in Kyiv to guide
his hands over the vast array of gleaming black
and white keys, and now the warm glow
of a single-stage light enveloped
the imposing nine-foot Steinway that brooded
like a *Toro Bravo* in the Iberian sunlight

and now there he was — a tall yet short-waisted man
walking slowly to the edge of the stage to pause
and bow and tell his audience this performance
would be for his mother, his first piano teacher

I didn't notice right away when he turned briskly
to move to the piano bench and position himself
all the way to one side — ungainly and not perfectly
lined up, awkward, but then again accentuated
by his hands tilted down, and palms slightly
below the level of the Steinway's gleaming
Bavarian spruce keys, nearly cupping the edge
playing chords with straight fingers
and always the little finger of his right hand
it was said, curiously curled up and ready
to strike like a cobra — I didn't notice
until he had started in, and then I spotted
that awkward gap, the place beside him, empty
but now for the ghost of his mother leading
her young son through the moment
guiding him in all the radiance of his return

In the Light of an Ordinary Morning

I study the ants
swarming the counter tops
in the light of an ordinary morning
Some march in single file
others in twos
Some pause momentarily
remembering suddenly
they left behind their wallet
or prescription
on the dresser at home
Some stand stock still
maybe waiting for a friend
maybe talking on the cell phone
Some scurry like they're late
for an appointment
Some walk in circles
confused and desolate over
a bad piece of news
A dab of strawberry jam
is the prize, the mother lode
It sits on the cutting board
amid toast crumbs
and the engineers are drafting
a strategy to spirit this
to the nest, to the Queen
who paces in front
of a tiny ant mirror
despairing over the weight
she's put on and what
she'll wear for the feast

celebrating their great find
I'm way ahead
I know something they don't
I know it's a matter of time
before I wreak havoc
upon this industrious colony
What shall it be?
Flood from an overturned mug?
Tsunami by wash cloth?
Death by a giant finger
flicking them into insect eternity?
Or should I be the benevolent god?
I'm way ahead —
Let them live an hour longer
while I drive to Home Hardware
and buy those tiny plastic
feeding stations
— space age looking drive-ins
I'll invite them one by one
to pull into these rest stops
along their route
to gorge themselves
on super-sized meal deals
I'll give them time to go back
and tell their friends
and bring the little ones,
the old, the sick
I'm way ahead of them
God is good
God is patient
God feeds his children

Final Portrait

Pat Sturn, renowned Canadian portrait
photographer on her death bed

Her right hand gripped the railing
of the hospital bed like someone
clinging to the last fragment
of a capsized and splintered boat

and I watched her sink ever
deeper into those last moments
poised and acquiescent
for new adventure

She was one hundred, curled up in the bed
like a breath-mark in a musical script
accentuating how her twisted johnny gown
tightened around her skeletal frailty
eyes shut and face gaping up

She knew what she was doing —
petitioning no prayers, no mourning

offering only this frighteningly tiny frame
and upturned face and bony fingers
clutching the cold rail
of the high bed near the tall west window

and having the blinds drawn up
the morning sunlight happily lit
her wispy white hair and sullen cheeks

— this, a signature pose, the final gesture
of this one-hundred-year-old portrait photographer

Rhubarb Pie in the Summer Kitchen

For James Reaney

It was easy to write
about him, riding
out there with a rhubarb pie
on the back of a bicycle
to the farmhouse
The tin roof calling out
in the afternoon heat
I expected him
to be at the screen door
or waving to me from the yard
I expected the black dog
running from the children
who played on the truck tire
swinging from the tired maple
that yielded obediently at each new demand
It was easy to write about him
because we would walk
out to the pond
ringed by the trees he planted
years ago and by the memories
of a childhood I'd read about
in his poems and plays
I thought it entirely appropriate
to bring the pie
entirely appropriate
that later we would sit
in the summer kitchen
for tea, that our voices
would wend their way through
the old house, and breathe
there a moment, tucked
away among the crumbling eaves

Walking Backwards on the Ambassador Bridge in 1937

The skinny boy folded his Assumption Church
baptismal certificate in half, stuffed it
into his pant pocket and hopped
into his uncle's big Oldsmobile
and rode to the Ambassador Bridge —
an early morning, clouds as big
as freighters floated in the high blue sky
and his uncle shook his head
in disbelief or scorn or whatever
at this whole idea that lay ahead

The boy stared at his shoes as they drove a mile
to the bridge, paid the toll and started
across, hardly any traffic this early
His uncle's car slowed and he looked over
saying not a word then smiled, and said
"Mom, told me …"
"Told you what?" he asked. "Get out
in the sunshine!" They laughed
and so it started, beginning his walk
across the Bridge on a sunny Sunday morning
a little cool but that was fine he thought
as he stepped out of his uncle's car
on the iron bridge and waved goodbye before
edging his way along, then he peered up
at the lofty girders, muttered a little prayer
his heart pumping so hard he believed
it might pop out of his chest like a trout in a stream

That first step, shaky, the bridge faintly swaying
or maybe he just imagined that, but he stepped
backwards, one, two, three, four, five and
now was on his way, yes, backwards, one
merry step at a time, the plan to slip all the way
across to Detroit, eyes front and soon passing him
were windshields of surprised faces, finger-pointing passengers
windows rolled down, curses and cheers and laughter
yet soon he was gaining momentum, grinning
widely, laughing inside, and picking up stride
and felt a little like his hero, Plennie Wingo
the Texas man who had set the world record
walking backwards from Los Angeles to Boston
and all through Europe, wearing out 12 pairs
of shoes, maybe not as crazy as the man
who sat atop a flagpole for 49 days or
the fellow who pushed a peanut up the 4,302 meter high
Pikes Peak in Colorado using only his nose
He felt good, felt like doing this, not on a whim
but like following a blueprint, like Wingo practicing
each day marching in reverse, mastering it first by sticking
to the backyard, parading along the fence
and past the garage and down the driveway
and back up and starting all over again
and finally said the hell with it and strutted
along Wyandotte past bakeries and shoe repair shops
and confectioneries and nobody really noticed at all
and he wished for those rear-view mirror goggles
Wingo used for his travels, even wrote to him
but never heard back and so he stepped out
that Sunday morning, a bit of a breeze
his felt cap yanked down tight in expectation
of an abrupt wind that might send it aloft

— he wasn't about to change the world
or anything, he was just going for a walk
and thought of it like his handwriting —
letters spilling out on that backward slant
straight across the page like nobody's business
and why resist the line that sent those words
like wild horses in the opposite direction
— it mattered nothing now that his world
was straight ahead, a single narrow line of the road
and the only sound these steady footsteps
and a prayer in his heart telling him
I'm going backwards to find myself

On First Hearing Gordon Lightfoot

Maybe the spring of 1967
on a cool Saskatchewan night
I was following the edge of the highway
daydreaming those flat open fields

maybe praying under an ink-black sky
that rested solitary and present over me
like the palm of a hand

when a preacher swerved
to the side of the road
in a dusty green *Plymouth Belvedere*

I spotted the flashing red of the ribbon style taillights
that wrapped around the knife-edge crease
running down to the bumper
and heard the man shout if I needed a ride

I hopped in, eager to be on my way
and talk soon turned to Jesus
and forgiveness and morality
and the Psalms
and I asked if he could turn on the radio

That's when I first heard that voice
sailing up and out this preacher's car —
a voice that spun in the still prairie air
the blur of notes like the landscape
whistling by

and I told him to turn up the radio
and that he'd have to stop talking and listen
and said if the apostles had this man's voice
there'd be real hope to cling to

and we wound the windows shut
and grew silent in that sudden moment
seeing the highway stretching clean and straight
beneath us like endless prayer

but we fell silent and alone as
that voice in the wilderness
was taking us somewhere different
somewhere distant

and maybe the dashboard lit up
like a votive lamp — I'm not sure

The Red Ribbon

For George E. Lee

I have tucked this red ribbon
inside my black notebook —
jottings about life
on the hospital ward
the nurses
visits from the surgeon
advice from the nutritionist
I scribbled out all the meds
given to me, the frequency
potential side effects
Noted all the blood work
done, the CT scan
X-rays and white blood cell scans
The red ribbon sits there
day after day — sent to me
by a Highgate sheep farmer
as a bookmark
First prize
Wallacetown Fair
Doesn't say which year
Doesn't say for what
I never win first prize
only ever second or third
or worse honorable mention
A watercolour when I was eight
fetched honorable mention
at the C.N.E.
It was dreadful —
a picture of a fellow fishing

along the Detroit River
He looked disfigured
Judges deemed it "inventive"
Now I have a first prize ribbon
from a town I know nothing about
a fair I've never been to
First prize
a shiny red ribbon
I imagine wearing it proudly
strolling amid the bustle
of farmers and housewives
flashing my first prize ribbon
pacing aisles of the best
apple pie, largest pumpkin
longest cucumber
standing about as 4-H club boys
and girls guide sheep and cows
one by one to parade
in the sunlit show grounds
of Wallacetown —
A Ferris wheel spins against
the blue sky, balloons
drift above the din
I imagine walking about with my red ribbon
first prize winner
top of my class
best of the best
my chest sporting the purest
red flower of Agricultural Fairs
I saunter into an exhibition hall
with rows and rows of cages
— chickens and roosters
winners and losers

red, blue, and yellow ribbons
festooned like Christmas lights
to narrow cages —
I think this is me
I walk about with my red ribbon
till I spot the losers — big sad eyes
of these birds
bewildered also-rans
melancholy shut-ins
and know I am one of them
I pick the best of the worst
— a dull white hen
with a gimpy leg
I love her eyes
mawkish and anxious
like women on 1960s
television's *Queen for a Day*
I love her eyes
and when she turns away
I quietly affix this radiant red ribbon
to her rickety cage

The Old Stables at Kenilworth Racetrack

That day driving out
to the tumbledown stables south of the city
I knew nothing of that moment in October 1920
I'd gone there with a woman I'd met at a bookstore
— horseback riding late, late afternoon
straw and dust and manure
the sharp odour of Absorbine and tobacco
and seeing threadbare plaid blankets folded
over the gates in the horse barn
and the final rays of sunlight
pouring into the stalls

I watched this quiet, elderly man leading the horses
out to the yard, the rich chestnut slope of their beauty
accentuated by late-fall light
I knew nothing of that moment so long ago
but think of it now, too late
and realize this man was there —
a boy among the stables
fetching straw and oats
his milky blue eyes and boyish hands
guiding the horses
into the silent moonlit yard at dawn

I want him to be there again with the great ones
— the race of the century
Man O'War and *Sir Barton*
I want him at the edges, slipping past
with pails of clean water
the sense of the stillness of the stall

where motionless Man O'War stood
— they say Big Red, as he was called,
was so beautiful it made you want to cry —
his very stillness was that
of a coiled spring, a crouched tiger

I want to believe Big Red scared the boy
that first morning in the fall
Yet I knew nothing of that day in October
when I drove out to those old stables
where this boy once stood in awe
of men who kept watch over the great stallion

I knew nothing of the track we rode on
at twilight where Big Red once galloped
like a nightmare roaring into history
I wished now I had paid attention
I wished I had remembered what this man
looked like, what he might've said
I wished now we could've spoken
Instead, I sat perched on a broken-down horse
trotting along a track I knew nothing about
trailing after a new girlfriend
thinking only of her
and my next move

The Art of Writing

That morning in the spring
we had to be the only ones on the lake
with a swarm of clouds in a sky above
like a brooding mother gathering us
into her warmth

I was too busy maybe to notice
as I carefully threaded my fishing line
all the while the solitary aluminum boat
ever hushed dipped in rhythmical pace
to the silent sway of the dark water

and my older brother's voice soon broke out
across the lake, echoing precise instructions
for my initiation into this artful practice
of angling smallmouth bass

I am not sure I heard him as I spun out
a line like a run on sentence with nowhere
to go but into the cool air cherishing only
the reckless wish for those green and black
takings to leap from the deep mysteries
of this sleeping lake

and yet nothing and nothing as the sun
elbowed its way past billowy stubborn clouds
to lift us into its presence and still nothing

I am not sure if I even cared now —
my thoughts gradually lured away
by the smoothed and mirrored lake with its gallery
of stately trees and clouds

when suddenly the line twitched and stiffened
and pulled and tugged again, and I began
to reel furiously, all certainty fixed in that instant
and there it was, the glory of a pumpkinseed sunfish
hurling itself into the cool air, its oily, wavy
blue-green stripes catching the first light of day
with unexpected splendour and luck and innocence

In that moment I was sure about everything

Chasing the Light

I must catch the moon
and run down the beach
to see it clearly
its path across the lake
in a straight line
like someone challenging me
to choose sides

I must catch the moon
as it rises above the forest
to see it clearly
its height stretching for darkness
in the boldest of its reach
like someone waking suddenly
for me to embrace

I must catch the moon
and race down along the river
to see it clearly
its face nodding sleepily
from behind a cloud
like an old man dreaming
the slow spinning of a night sky

I must catch the moon
as it moves like sunlight on a street
to see it clearly
its captive gesture telling me
to trust its graceful dance

Let Me Go First

I don't want to mourn your death
Let me go first, free me of arrangements
solemnities, eulogies, loneliness, closets full of shoes
and dresses, jewelry, eyeglasses

Let me be the flattened bicycle tire
hanging from a nail in the garage
an abandoned, forgotten tennis racket
a winter tire leaning against a post
a cardboard box of old vinyl records

I'd rather be those than be me
waiting to catch up, days spent writing
sappy sentimental poems to your memory

I know it's selfish but what else is new —
I was always first out the door
you always minutes late

I don't want to change things —
I just want to be first

P.S. I still love you

Acknowledgements

I am one of lucky ones to have such stellar mentors early in my career as Miriam Waddington, Morley Callaghan, Al Purdy, and James Reaney. They graciously read my work and told me the truth. I learned from them, and continue to learn from so many others including Micheline Maylor, Christopher Lawrence Menard, Mary Ann Mulhern, André Narbonne, Phil Hall, Rosemary Sullivan, Peter Hrastovec, Douglas MacLellan, Michael Mirolla, Madelyn Della Valle, Howard and Jeannette Aster, Terry Ann Carter, Karen Mulhallen, Susan McMaster, Dan Wells, and so many more. The poems in this book are gathered up over 50 years from journals, magazines, anthologies, and from collections of mine from several Canadian publishing houses most notably Mosaic Press, Biblioasis Books and Guernica Editions. My thanks to them for believing in my work. My gratitude also goes to the editors of this collection, John B. Lee and Bruce Meyer for their insights and guidance. I must also acknowledge the work of Julienne Rousseau and Kalie Chapman for helping me assemble this book. Of course, without the support and trust of my family, these poems never would have been written.

About the Author

Marty Gervais is a Canadian poet, journalist, photographer, and teacher. He has won many literary awards, including the prestigious Toronto's Harbourfront Festival Prize for his contributions to Canadian letters and to emerging writers. Gervais is also the recipient of 16 Western Ontario Newspaper Awards for journalism, the Milton Acorn People's Poetry Prize, the Queen's Jubilee Medal, and was Windsor's inaugural Poet Laureate.

Printed by Imprimerie Gauvin
Gatineau, Québec